The Adventure of Michelle, Hillary and Jesse
The Conversation

Ng Dagreat

AuthorHouse™ UK
1663 Liberty Drive
Bloomington, IN 47403 USA
www.authorhouse.co.uk
UK TFN: 0800 0148641 (Toll Free inside the UK)
UK Local: 02036 956322 (+44 20 3695 6322 from outside the UK)

This book is printed on acid-free paper.

ISBN: 978-1-6655-8564-4 (sc)
       978-1-6655-8565-1 (e)

Print information available on the last page.

Published by AuthorHouse 02/09/2021

authorHOUSE®

ACT ONE
Scene 1

BY

Ng Dagreat

(She quickly picks her two-year-old up and checks his mouth with her finger to ascertain what he had in his mouth)

Hillary: Oh, this boy!!, he shouted!

Michelle: I do not know why he will pick up things from the floor.

Mum: Well, toddlers and babies learn when they eat toys and stuff, but he will outgrow that stage. Please, Michelle, get me the changing bag okay.

Michelle: Okay, Mummy.

Hillary: I want a cup of drink!

Michelle: Why did you not request for a juice when we were downstairs?

Hillary: Can I make the drink myself Mummy?

Mummy: Get me the changing bag first for Jesse, we can discuss your drink.

Michelle: I have told him to make a drink himself, so he should leave me alone.

Mummy: He was speaking to me and not you.

Michelle: Where is the changing bag?

(Shouting from the next room).

Mummy: Do not worry your pretty head Michelle, Hillary has got it.

Michelle: Where is it then?

Mummy: It is not downstairs, Michelle, can't you hear me? Hillary has given it to me.

(Mum was changing Jesse and spoke to him with a smile on her face).

Mum: Hi, Jesse boy and how are you?

(Jesse is smiling and making the 'coo' sound! Hillary and Michelle stomp into the room, arguing over the Juice).

Hillary: What! where is my Juice?

Michelle: Why did you not tell me that you needed a cup of Juice when we were downstairs?

Mummy: Please no more arguments, go and change into your pajamas, and I will get everyone milk and biscuit.

(with Jesse shouting now at the background as the little chat with Mummy had stopped when she tried to settle the argument between Michelle and Hillary).

Mummy: Who will throw away the dirty nappy for me in the bin, please?

Hillary: Me, Me!

(Mum hands over the nappy to Hillary)

Mummy: Thank you, Hillary. Please wash your hands afterwards.

Hillary: You are welcome, Mummy.

(Michelle laughing sarcastically).

Michelle: I will never be a volunteer for that disgusting thing! I will never (she was laughing).

Hillary: Ah, ah, ah!

Michelle: Switch on the light if you cannot see the bin.

Mummy: You cannot volunteer for such a disgusting thing, but someone did yours when you were a baby. I do not want to hear that again.

(Michelle smiled and cheekily covered her face. Mum is speaking to Jesse, who is now cooing and smiling).

Mummy: Is Jesse, boy, okay?

Jesse smiles at her as she tickles him, and she smiled back at him.

Michelle: Mummy, today, Jesse covered his face with his clothe and smiled at me. He crawled up to me with smiles and ran back to the bed to cover his face.

Mum: I saw him, and he was smiling at you too.

Mummy and Michelle started laughing at the trick Jesse pulled out earlier today. She told Michelle that it is not pleasant for a baby to cover his face for too long to avoid a respiratory problem.

Mummy: I do not know who taught Jesse that. Did you teach him the trick, Michelle?

Michelle: No, not at all. It was not me. He tried to take off his clothes, and it covered his face, and I turned to look at him. Then, I pulled his t-shirt down. He was now smiling and looking at me.

(Mummy and Michelle were smiling).

Mummy faced Jesse and said:

Mummy: So, Jesse, you are now playing Peekaboo with yourself. That's very wise of you.

(Michelle joined Mummy to smile and Michelle)

Michelle: Jesse is starting Pre-school, aren't you, Jesse?

You will go to primary school, secondary school, and the university. You can become a professor.

(Jesse was smiling and sounded very excited as Mummy and Michelle spoke and touched him on the cheek and feet).

Mum: Lesson learnt

Remember that a baby will grow from going to school to preschool, nursery, primary, university and till any level they eventually desire.

Mum: It is time to read your bedtime story.

Michelle and Hillary: Yeah!

Michelle, Hillary and Jesse looked very excited when Mum brought out the new storybook titled.

'The Little Princess

by

Ng Dagreat'

*T*here is a little princess who lived in a town named Mecca.

Mecca was a city situated in a country named London. The little Princess was the only child of her parents, and she lived in a big mansion in the City. The Princess is not a proud child but respects her elders and friends. Despite her father's status quo, she stayed humble and friendly to their maids and parents' workers.

One day, the little Princess had a dream where she became very famous through her drawings and illustrations.

She woke up and told her maid. Her maid said to her that she could not become famous because of her age. The little Princess felt sad and wondered why Lisa, her maid, will say such a thing.

'What does it take to be famous she asked herself!'

'I love to draw, and my teachers tell me that I am the best'.

Maybe Lisa is right. I am just a ten-year-old girl and may not be able to manage it.

'I wish I can become famous one day and the world will see my beautiful colours and how I can illustrate through drawings.' She said'

One fateful day, the little Princess got to school, and Mrs. Henry announced that

'A competition was going on in Egypt for all the schools. It is for pupils who love to draw'. If you are interested, please submit your illustrations to Mr. Adam with your name on it. May I remind everyone that this competition can bring good fame for the pupil and the school? Thank you'

The little Princess was excited, but she refused to tell anyone that she had some drawings she could submit. She thought no one believes in her, so she compiled her illustration and introduced the next day to Mr. Adam.

After school hours that evening, she could not sleep.

'Are you okay' Princess asked Rebecca the Mum.

Yes, Mummy, I am okay, replied Princess.

'But you look worried and not settled.'

'yes and no Mum'.

'What do you mean yes and no.'

'I enrolled in a competition with my illustrations, and I hope I win as that could make me famous.'

'hahaha laughed Rebecca, my little princess wants to be the best and famous.'

'yes, Mum.'

'but your Dad and Mum are famous.'

'You are the only daughter of the King of Mecca, and you should be proud of yourself.'

'I know Mum', but that is different.'

'I love to draw, and I want to be known for it. The competition is not just within Mecca but beyond other parts of the world.'

'what a big dream you have princess' she laughs.

'I wish you all the best darling', but you have to go to bed now.'

'Thank you, Mum, I am glad you believe in me.'

'Of course darling, you are the best in everything.'

Princess hugged her Mum, and she went to bed happy knowing that someone believes in her dream.

'I wonder why Lisa did not sound too great about her drawing? Could she be jealous? her daughter Kenny did not seem very great in her studies.'

'well, I will focus on what my Mum said'.

On the 20th of March, that year. Everyone gathered in assembly for the Headteacher's speech, and she said that School Road Model primary was the best for the drawing competition. Everyone seemed very excited and wondered who it was. Princess did not tell her friends, so, no one asked her if she was the winner.

She could not believe her ears. She was not aware that the results would be this quick.

The winner of the most famous and best drawings is The Princess of Mecca from P5.

Everyone screamed with a loud noise. Donna and Ashley, Princess good friends, were surprised and thought Princess was secretive because she did not tell anyone about the drawing.

'The Headteacher gave an announcement in class for anyone who was interested said Princess'

'But you should have told us so that we can try.'

'Well, you all know I love to draw, and I have never seen you drawing before.'

'Can the Princess of Mecca from the P5 class step out for us to celebrate her bravery?'

Princess left her friends, who did not seem very pleased with her success and went to the stage.

The Head Teacher shook her hands and told her to make a speech.

'I am grateful for this day as I have long desired for people to know me for what I do.'

'My advice to anyone here is that you should never give up on your dreams.

Some people may not believe in you and others will. Follow your instinct, and remember that one day you will become famous and respected all over the world for good'.

Her talk was on all television and Lisa- the maid watched her speech at the assembly while she cleaned her room.

'wow, see little princess has made it with her drawings; her good dreams came true'. I must inform her majesty immediately.

The End.

Michelle, Hillary and Jesse had slept off while Mum read the story.

Mum quickly covered them up and said Goodnight with a kiss on their cheek.

Printed in the United States
by Baker & Taylor Publisher Services